COWBOY GENES
AND OTHER STORIES

COWBOY GENES

AND OTHER STORIES

WES LEE

Grist Books 2014

Editor Michael Stewart

Editorial Team Danni Hodson-Michael, Sophie Johnson, Emma
Marsden, George Taylor

Cover Design Kagayaku Ink

Inner Page Design Carnegie Book Production

Cowboy Genes and other stories is published by Grist Books.

www.hud.ac.uk/grist

Grist Books is supported entirely by The University of
Huddersfield and would not exist without this support.
We would like to take the opportunity to express our gratitude
for this continuing support.

ISBN: 978-0-9563099-3-8

University of
HUDDERSFIELD
Inspiring tomorrow's professionals

for Richard who believes

Contents

Cowboy Genes

I N THE MONTHS after I nearly died I read Westerns. There was something about setting out on a journey over untamed, dangerous country that appealed. The laconic cowboys. The fearless Indians. I found the clichés comforting. The stories didn't demand too much and they had a heart. A heart and finding a way back were my concerns, and Westerns seemed to deliver them in spades.

After the botched operation, what the doctors called my medical misadventure, what I liked to call the massacre, I'd fled Sydney with my husband Max, jettisoning possessions along the trail – an oak sideboard, matching ebony corner cabinets, a kauri dressing table with a huge oval mirror – useless furniture that would only weigh us down. We'd rented a place in the Blue Mountains, a house with a vantage point. I was able to see for miles which was fitting in a way. It felt like an Apache mesa, or a Yankee fort, being up so high and in a reasonably protected position. Max had said it was a place where we could re-group, make some sense out of what had happened, but I thought of it as circling our wagons.

I was in pain. I couldn't walk very far. The doctors couldn't tell me what had happened during the appendectomy to cause so much pain, other than I had gone into cardiac arrest under the gas and they had to fight to bring me back. They mumbled things about scarring, and giving it time – that these things happen.

You'll be happy to know there is no lasting damage to your heart.

It was winter and I was cold most of the time. I couldn't sleep unless I wore wool against my skin, much like the long johns that cowboys sleep, shag and die in. I was frozen out on the prairie, I felt like I'd crossed a thousand miles. I was a shivering thing waiting to be born, not knowing if it would ever happen: if things would get warm, natural and easy again.

I moved from the bedroom to the sunroom in the afternoon, lay on the day-bed and got lost on other people's trails, in other people's dreams and adventures, in other people's sorrow and pain. I rode with a cowboy named Tracy Beets, across the Texas panhandle. Out in the desert, leading my appaloosa past red, alien-shaped mesas. Fording rivers. Huddled around a fire at night, singing mournful tunes and listening for sounds out of kilter – the call that might be an Indian, but was probably a bird. Or something we'd kill and eat the next day when we moved along the trail.

In Westerns, life was short and full of pain – pleasure had to be grasped when you could get it. Death was often an accidental affair, hit by a stray bullet shot in the air while celebrating a win at the card table. The heartless sting of a rattlesnake bite. Life was full of misadventure. Things just happened and they happened quick, you knew you could be killed at any time.

At night, a skinned mule panted through my dreams, bleeding and raw-boned, a hideous wounded thing, its black eyes staring. I knew it had been sent by something stunned and struggling at the centre of me to make some sense of the massacre. Trying to find some language for what had happened to me under the gas. Why didn't you resist? Why didn't you fight that cold-eyed stranger wearing a mask? The skinned mule asked, tongue lolling, pounding past, turning back to look at me with spite in its eye.

When I tried to call friends back in Sydney, they wanted to know why I had left so quickly. Why did you move all the way out there? Why didn't you tell anyone you were leaving? They wanted to know things that didn't seem important to me. They wanted to know why I was still sick if I hadn't lost an arm, a leg, a baby.

'Are you paralysed?'

'I'm in a lot of pain.'

'But your heart's okay?'

'I've got scarring... inside...'

'Where inside?'

'The doctors don't know.'

'What do you do out there alone all day?'

'I read Westerns.'

'God, I haven't had time to read a book in years, why are you reading those things?'

They would listen for awhile, then start in with their tales of woe. How the fettuccine had stuck to the bottom of the pan and they'd had to scrape it off with a knife. How things had broken down: the car, the toaster, the butter conditioner. How there were never enough minutes in the day. Their lives had stayed the same, while mine had changed. I imagined Sara tapping on the telephone table as she spoke to me, scribbling something on the shopping list, circling the dates on the calendar when she would ovulate and later mourn the blood that would appear at its allotted hour, as regular and steadfast as her heartbeat. Or Amanda, sitting at her desk antici-pating happy-hour, conjuring margaritas, the buzz of salt on her tongue, sinking into the frisson of the night she was planning.

They wanted to make idle chat, while I wanted some-thing monumental, something they couldn't possibly give. I wanted some relief, a whisper that would make it all go away. I wanted them to speak like the cowboys I'd been spending my days with.

You were lucky then you became unlucky, Beets had told his friend Solly when he lay ill with fever; his eyes holding his in the glow of the campfire. Beets had fed him broth from a spoon, urging him to drink so he would not die. Keeping vigil through the long nights, covering him with a buffalo hide.

People come back from the dead at their own pace, Beets had told Solly when he'd tried to recover too quickly and get back on his horse.

His words had resounded within me. I loved the hokeyness, the straight delivery, the space he left for mystery. His easy smile. His soul, there on his face for everyone to see. I loved how he would stare off into the distance and not say anything. I understood how he would just disappear. A cowboy rode off and no one asked him where he was going or when he'd be back. It was a man's right to be free, angry, afraid, joyous. In Westerns, a man let another man be.

The cowboys respected silence, a man who talked too much was not to be trusted. I had become intimate with silence. I had come up close to silence, spending the daylight hours alone, staring out of the windows at a landscape that looked like it had been shocked – caught roaring in mid-motion like an icy black frieze.

Max would arrive back in the dark, his headlights winding up the drive. Coming home to a quiet house. Sometimes I pictured him getting out of the car and just standing, staring through the stained glass panel in the front door, trying to make out my shape in the low light inside. I'd see him turn away, turn back, get in the car and drive. But he always walked in. He'd fix dinner, sit across from me, his eyes bright and steady, waiting out the dry spell with the heart of a cowboy, a man watching for rain coming over the mountains, waiting for the weather to break.

In bed, when Max reached out for me, I wanted to make reassuring sounds, I wanted to make the noises I used to make to fold him into me. I wanted to brush back his hair, I wanted to let him touch me. But my body had become a desert.

'When things get better,' I'd hear him say as we lay in the dark, 'We'll go somewhere.'

He kept talking about going on holiday, he kept talking about things that were going to happen. I could see he spent his days in the sunlit times before it all got cloudy.

I envied him that he could get away, drive to the safety of the office. He could find some relief, talk to people about ordinary things. He didn't have to consider his body, it wasn't a broken thing – a mewling, injured kitten that wheedled and cringed. I imagined his office like a warm cocoon – people laughing while they poured coffee out of the coffee machine. The simplest, easiest human contact had become alien to me. I felt if I opened my mouth, pain would flow out. The imagined workers would scurry away when I approached the water-cooler, raising their eyebrows at each other.

'It's not fair,' Max kept saying, over and over.

I didn't know if he was speaking about me.

'It's not as if you're in a wheelchair… you're not an invalid, Gina,' my father told me when I called him in Dublin. He was more interested in my mother's labrador, Molly, how she had suddenly gone off her food.

'She doesn't give a crap about my damn dog…' I could hear my mother slurring in the background.

When it came to kin, I had the classic Western profile – a stoic martyr for a daddy and a drunk for a mother who spent her days bitter at the neck of a bottle.

I came from the right stock. I had the genes to be a cowboy.

'Tell her she's the one who's selfish… tell her she thinks she knows everything!' my mother shouted.

'Your mother says you've developed a talent for running away.'

He was her foot soldier. A spear carrier, who backed her up under pain of death. They were a gang. I often thought about what would happen if he went first. I pictured her weakened and alone.

'I'm in pain, daddy…'

'I can't help you, Gina.'

'But…'

'No! Gina.'

I could hear him breathing out there in the suburbs, nursing a thousand hurts.

'You're lucky you can just give up,' he whispered.

When things got so bad on the frozen prairie, when the winter hemmed them in, the cowboys talked about taking their own lives, better that than be hung over a Comanche fire and tortured, or picked by buzzards when they fell on the trail and could be carried no further. Solly put a gun to his eye and blew out the back of his skull, killing himself instantly. Beets found him dead in the morning, his clothing frozen to his skin. He accepted it. He didn't see it as a shameful thing. He buried him in a mound piled with rocks, said a prayer over him.

And like that cowboy I thought I wouldn't get through the winter. His face had seemed like a lovely dream to me. I wanted to give up, just fall asleep on the prairie curled up beside him and not wake up, twisted in a zigzag shape, my lashes frosted with ice.

But the spring came, cracking things open. A blue haze settled around the mountains. The sun belted down, pushing out seeds and berries, setting things in motion, sending things stirring. I dragged an armchair outside and let the sun wash over me. The skinned mule stopped visiting me in my dreams.

Max would find me there when he got home, asleep out on the veranda, a book lying on the deck that had tumbled from my hands.

In Westerns, the change of winter to spring was something cowboys prayed for. It was the divide between life and death. When weather really meant something.

One afternoon I touched my body for the first time since the massacre. With the spring sounding out and my fingers circling, I crossed over a threshold into a place that I thought I had forgotten. A world buried in me that opened like a bud.

Diseases
From Space

'**R**EMEMBER THAT TERRIBLE man our mother hated?'
'Our father,' I said.
'Yes.'

It was David's familiar greeting, the delivery as seemingly casual as Hi, or Hello, or Hey.

There had always been darkness in him. I tried to read what level it was at. It's the kind of habit you develop – watching for signs, waiting for things to unravel, push to the surface.

Our mother had taken off her clothes and stood in the rain. She stood on the banks of rivers, stretched on her toes, flung her arms open. She stood amongst trees where she told us that space dust falls, 'Where particles congregate, so thick they land – a tongue's scraping... a morning tongue.' She'd pushed her tongue out at us when we were children to emphasise her point.

'I heard you could catch diseases from space, I was hoping to get one,' she told the cops when they found her. We'd imagined them capturing her in a big net, a butterfly net, running along riverbanks in the rain and finally swooping her up as she ran laughing in front of them. She'd run so fast, like an athlete.

But instead of catching diseases from space she got hypothermia, and had to be taken to one of those places.

There are lots of glamorous mental institution stories – my mother's isn't one of them. Stories reported by writers/artists/poets with dry acerbic voices, as if all that time, on the far reaches of sanity, they'd been swivelling an olive in a dirty martini, commenting on what they saw in the ward around them – creating this great, rolling ironic distance, a fog between them and everything else.

Institution porn, David called it: my holiday in hell, I observed things and brought them back: people with interesting afflictions and inflections, ways of speaking duly reported, scribbled fast in the margins. Only, anyone who has really been there doesn't feel like a reporter.

'You just feel scared all of the time,' David had told me. 'We don't glamorize our lost hours in the burnt-out edges of the room. But we might, given a lot of distance, make it funny for other people. Isn't that what we all do in the end, turn it into a joke?... I made friends there, but not ones you could keep, the friendships don't last unless you're heading back there.'

And now he was out again.

Our mother had painted herself gold like Cleopatra and walked through a shopping mall as proud as any Egyptian Queen. Our father had floated in a bath of blood.

I imagined David in that same bath. And me coming home, the house in darkness. Would I smell it when I entered the house? I knew I would. I'd recognize it. I'd know that smell anywhere. But if I couldn't smell it – if it didn't hit my tongue, register at the back of my throat – I wouldn't know there was something wrong, and walking into the bathroom, not knowing, my knees giving way – could he give me another moment like that?

The least he could do was prepare me for it, spread some of his blood around before the life left him. Spatter it in the hallway, rub it along the doors. Then I'd know when I walked in the house, I'd smell it in the air. Then I'd be ready.

The things you can never say to each other: *will you leave signs, a few little clues to break the shock… because David, my little heart can't take it.*

It's the kind of raw, black acerbic thing they say to each other in those institution stories.

David lights a cigarette, the tips of his fingers dark and bitten. His eyes sunken. His body fat from institution food. Too much gravy, too many potatoes, too much comfort food.

'Did you see The Matrix?'

'Yes,' I said.

'Wasn't it great that The Oracle smoked?'

'Everybody liked that.'

'*He* smoked.'

'Who smoked?'

'That terrible man our mother hated.'

I'd never seen him smoke.

There are things the younger one never sees – that only the older one is privy to. The younger one can sometimes live their life in bliss, but sometimes the younger one is the one who doesn't escape.

'It was a secret,' David whispered.

And then he laughed. I loved his laugh, he laughed through his teeth, the tip of his tongue just visible between them. A hissing, gulping kind of laugh. His eyes alive in that moment. I wanted always to see that laugh.

11

'What will you do?' I asked him.

'I might go on a trip somewhere.'

'Where would you like to go?'

'The past.'

'You really should write something, you'd be good at it.'

And then I remembered all the other people I'd known that would be good at something.

'Yeah?'

'It's in our genes... at least it should be.'

'There was this half Irish, half Albanian guy on the ward...'

'Is this a joke?'

'He told me his mother had been six foot tall with bright red hair. She'd beaten the crap out of his philandering, sex-crazed father every Saturday night, and I was amazed at the bland, watered-down person they'd produced... These hot mixes of people often spawn these blurred-out offspring... it's the combustible mix of the couple itself that's exciting.'

David had told the doctors he'd seen potatoes turn into spiders – spider legs had grown from their eyes, twitching around like witches' whiskers. He kept talking about a fish: a deep sea one with black pebble eyes and a long antenna baited with a light out in front of it, 'Like a donkey with a carrot to drive it forward. A fucking fish with a light in front of it... you can't tell me something didn't have a hand in that!'

He'd told them God had shown him evolution was a crock of shit. He'd seen God's hand in everything, and he knew he didn't need to be afraid. And then they'd taken that away (whispered that it wasn't true), and he'd been afraid, again. 'Inject me with a fairy tale, pure fucking fairy dust, pure glittering fairy smack... put it here!' he'd kept whacking his veins as they tried to lead him out of my house. And then he was out, mouth slack, tongue lolling, dead to the world – their drugs were good like that.

'I wish...' I said and stopped quickly.

I wish it could be different.

Sometimes the most simple sentences feel the best. So why can't we say them?

Some people say that one pain can lessen another. Like a lull between traffic. A car goes by and we breathe again. *Breathing*. Sitting together in café after café, David and I breathing together between pauses, between cars going by. All those memories and pauses. Smiling at each other with that terrible brimming sadness underneath.

'Remember that holiday – the drive to Blackpool?' David said.

'Two tires blew out in the pouring rain.'

'He got drenched changing the first. When the other one burst there was no spare.'

'And those were the good times.'

'Stuck by the side of the road, sleeping with him in the back of the station wagon, and you in the petrol station with her all night eating Mars bars.'

'We had to keep buying something or they'd throw us out.'

'In the cold?'

'Yes.'

'I was jealous of you in there. Stuck in the car with the windows all fogged, but now I'm glad. I remember his smell, and the lights... you never see those lights now... those up-all-night-outside-when-you're-a-child kind of lights. When everything is alive, happening around you and it's all unnamed. So big and there and constant.'

He stopped speaking.

'You only ever have one night like that and all the others that never come close, run into it,' he said.

'I remember counting Christmas trees from the car windows.'

'I lost count. I don't think I really liked counting even then.'

You might know by now that we actually loved that terrible man that our mother hated. We lost him when we lost her. She hated him for trying to stop her from doing 'hurtful' things. The sadness of that man and his great love for our mother is too much to bear without the blackness of that joke – without that edge to teeter on. David always skating on that edge. And me willing him not to leave, but when have wishes ever worked?

The last poem our mother wrote, she called, Dog in Concrete:

paw
then
paw
then
paw
a happy careless jig recorded
you can follow it
like a sentence
as it breaks
into a trot

You might think a person who wrote a poem like that was happy, but it's not the case. You only have to look at the lives of poets – how their hearts soar in a different way to our dull hearts. They can think they're Jesus, or an Egyptian Queen, they can run over hills and lose themselves in things we cannot hear.

'My little heart will give out,' she always said. And it had. Eventually. On the banks of rivers where space dust fell. Where particles congregate, launched from meteorites, drifting down, coating leaves, and our mother – standing with her arms flung wide – welcoming space dust in.

Sunspots

I TELL EVERYONE I was born in the year of the Tiger. Only my sisters know I'm really an Ox.

Eva's slim, white hands mime the tiger's mask around my face. She says she can see my mask slipping. Her fingers are soft as if she keeps them in gloves, perfumed and manicured and folded in a drawer. Yet I've seen burn marks on her hands from splashes of cooking oil or Lapsang Souchong that she's left brewing too long on the stove.

'Why don't you want to be an Ox?' she asks.

'Tigers are mercurial and dangerous.'

'But the Ox is sturdy and watchful.'

Octavio sits on the kitchen window ledge while Eva tapes anti-vivisection images to his cat dish – grainy photographs of kittens with electrodes embedded in their brains.

'No more baby birds or else,' she wags her finger in front of his face.

Octavio has that bored look that all cats have. Her finger is too slow. He's only animated by the dart of tail feathers or the twisting mid-air, death leap of a mouse. Fascination for a cat comes in the form of unpredictable movements.

Eva tells me I could never look after a cat, so she gives me goldfish for my birthday. When one of them dies, Eva stares at the coils of fish shit winding out from some invisible opening underneath its tail.

'We don't really change,' Eva says, 'we just get big and then get small again and then we're gone.'

She slaps a fat wedge of steak onto a smoking skillet, she's angry at me for killing her fish. When she gave me the fish, knowing she was going to die, everything hinged on keeping it alive.

~

When we were teenagers, Eva moved to Darwin. She used to send me presents in the mail. When something arrived, it usually signalled some kind of romantic crises – either she'd left someone or met someone. The larger, more exotic gift meant something had begun. When something had ended, the offerings were thin and flaky.

When she met Stefano, she sent me a comb carved out of boxwood with an inlaid, abalone trim. It smelt like a freshly opened coconut, the wood looked dark and oily. I tossed the comb into the bathroom drawer with all of the other gifts.

'Are you serious?' I remember asking her over the phone.

'It's really not an issue.'

'You hated pornography.'

'That was just a phase I went through.'

'Has he got *you* on film?'

'I'm the strawberry blond who gets burnt in the sun. There are lots of guys who really get into seeing peeling skin. Stefano gets off on seeing my nipples cracked.'

'That's crap,' I told her.

I sensed her finger hovering over the End button on her cellphone. I could hear her breathing out there on the rim of the lucky country.

'Do what you want,' I said.

'I will do what I want,' her voice had a desperate high note. An uncertain tremor.

Do what you want, I whispered as I clicked off my cellphone and threw it out into the sea.

Eva had booked the next flight out of Darwin before my cellphone had bumped onto the bottom of the Atlantic. She'd sped towards me. Chewing up scenery. Swooping across oceans like a vampire in a B-grade movie directed by an ex-advertising hack.

Eva arrived through the terminal gate shouting – carrying on the fight from where we'd left off. Her skin burnt, her hair too bright, in clothes unsuitable for a cold climate.

Our sister, Marla, had got out of bed early in Eva's honour, like a maid arriving in the dark to make sure the water was hot. Each morning she'd make an inventory of my kitchen in anticipation of Eva's every need.

'Tell us about where you're living?' Marla would ask.

And Eva would answer. Her garden filled with passionfruit flowers. Her potbelly pig tethered on the edge of the rainforest with a chain.

When I looked at Marla I could see she wasn't listening. She was thinking of the moment when she would stand at Heathrow and watch Eva's back moving away from her. Marla would take photographs until the plane became a small, black mark on the sky. And later, in the spare room, I knew she'd smell the crumpled dressing gown that Eva had let fall on the floor around her.

~

19

'It's not your fault. She wanted you to kill that fish, then she could blame you,' Marla tells me when we meet for coffee.

When two out of the three sisters are together the absent one is stretched over the table and pierced with bamboo. Eva sits at the apex of our triangle and there is much time spent flaying the peeled-back eyelids and repeatedly poking underneath the fingernails of the pale goddess.

Now, some of the pleasure leaks out around the edges. We catch ourselves looking around as if we're already speaking ill of the dead.

'She's so controlling,' Marla tells me.

'She's a monster.'

Our words seem kind of whispery and empty, not charged with the thrill they once had. Sometimes we can only repeat each other's phrases.

'She's a monster.'

'She'll outlast us.'

'She's a monster.'

'She'll outlast us.'

And when we laugh, it's full of weight like a chain dragging.

~

Octavio's eyes are a yellow blur through the distortion of the fish tank. He blinks at me and then he's gone.

Eva sits watching snails crawling in a line down a single strand of oxygen weed.

'At least you'll never have to be an old woman,' Marla tells her.

Marla hates old women. She fights her way out into the aisle if they sit beside her on the bus. She holds her breath when they walk past her in the supermarket, as if the air around them is contaminated.

'I hate their skinny old necks,' Marla says.

'I hate the sticky hands of children,' Eva says.

'Witches hate the smell of children,' I tell her.

Eva shrugs and takes a drag of her cigarette. She has a particular way of placing it in the nearby ashtray. She squashes it with two fingers, hard on the rim as if she is forcing it to stay there. The gesture seems magnified to me. I have become hyper-aware of her movements. They flare-up in the little kitchen like sunspots.

There is a photograph on the bench of Eva and Stefano on their honeymoon. The image has a radiance that could trick you into thinking that life is holy – something other than the dull thud of flesh meeting flesh. Turned towards one another in the breath before they kiss, their eyes are tunnels meeting.

'I bought the biggest steaks at the supermarket,' Eva says as she hefts the iron skillet out from underneath the bench. She becomes absorbed in a task quickly. When she cooks she enters another world.

'Not the tenderest steaks, not the soft morsels of fillet, but the biggest steaks,' she says.

I watch the way she strikes the match to light the gas. The way she blows it out and flicks it into the rubbish tin. I watch her turn and open the fridge with its rows of pills in the butter conditioner. Her clothes don't fit her properly anymore. I can see the bumps of her spine pushing up through her T-shirt, her jeans barely held up by her hips. I want to reach out and brush my finger over the tiny strawberry blond hairs on her forearm as she reaches into the fridge for the steaks.

'I don't want to get old,' Marla says.

'You will want to,' Eva tells her.

Eva calls me on the phone, crying in the middle of the night.

'You are the one I can call... you're the one who'll understand.'

She asks me to come over. It's three in the morning but I get in my car and drive. She has this idea about me that I don't sleep – she gives you a label and that's what you are forever. Marla is manic depressive and I'm an anorexic insomniac.

You never eat, she says when she cooks me the largest steak in her freezer. *And you never sleep.*

But I was sleeping when the telephone rang.

Sometimes she wakes me out of a dream. Once when she rang I jumped out of bed and ran into the wall, as if I'd been on full alert waiting for the phone to ring.

You don't eat and you don't sleep.

When I get to her house she's sitting at the kitchen bench crying. She's surrounded by Barbie dolls that Stefano has taken from a tenant in lieu of her rent that was overdue. She's brushing the long red hair of a Barbie in a silver dress. She gives me the comb and asks me to get out some of the tangles. I pick up a blond Barbie in a dress that has pressed too much flesh and start to comb.

She says she's crying for the tenant's daughter.

I don't ask her why she is in possession of the daughter's inheritance. I ask her where Stefano is in the middle of the night.

'Sleeping,' she says.

~

Eva cooks octopus in its own ink. She spends two days preparing Peking duck. Octavio is growing fat from all the titbits she puts in his bowl.

Marla and I sit in Eva's kitchen chain-smoking cigarettes.

'The duck will be beautiful,' Eva tells Octavio. She pushes the fur on his head until it's standing up the wrong way. 'You are a funny little man.'

When Eva returned from Darwin permanently – a strip of her hair had turned white. 'It's from the shock,' Eva told us when she got off the plane. 'Never let anyone give you a diagnosis.'

Stefano carried her bags as she walked through the terminal.

The white in her hair has disappeared now she has started to dye it.

When I stopped drinking, pale ridges appeared on the moons of my fingernails that took months to edge toward my fingertips. *I think when they've grown out you'll be cured,* Marla told me when she was going through one of her manic spells.

Eva's fingernails look pink and healthy. If she wasn't slowly shrinking there would be few signs of the shadows she's seen creeping through her lungs.

'I want you to take Octavio,' Eva says to Marla.

It's the first time she's said anything about what she wants to happen when she dies.

Marla says nothing. I watch her lips tremble – pulling from side to side against her will.

Eva puts a small copper pan on the stove. She measures out three teaspoons of Lapsang Souchong then drops the dark little twigs into the water. When she lights the element she leans on the kitchen bench and stares at me as she pushes her cigarette into the ashtray.

~

'Don't you drop me!' Eva shouts down the telephone line in the middle of the night. 'I won't let you drop me!'

'I'm not going to drop you,' I tell her.

But I do drop her.

I throw rocks into the ocean.

I listen to reports from Marla.

I stay out in the cold.

Then, after a short absence, I return with flowers. Stefano has painted the hallway a hot slick of orange that snakes toward her bedroom. I stand shaking at her door.

'You! You!' she screams.

She wants to fight, so I fight with her.

I fight until the sky turns dark. I fight until I'm allowed into the white light of the bedroom. Until she smooths out the beaten flowers and puts them in a vase.

The Gardenia Girls

I RIS AND I were wicked girls. We put lipstick on when we pulled up outside his house, admiring ourselves in the rear vision mirror while he watched. Knowing he was watching, we laughed and elbowed each other out of the way to get a better view of our own lips.

Hot pink is an inviting colour. There's no misinterpreting hot pink. It suited Iris's lips. She was the good-looking one with lips that people said were generous. My lips were thin and I knew bright colours just accentuated the thinness, but I always wore the same lipstick as Iris.

We might as well have been shouting taunts with that lipstick. Come over here, big boy! We want you, Mister! That's the kind of thing that goes through men's heads. It doesn't take much to set them off, just a glance, an intake of breath walking past them in the street. A finger raised to your hair could cause a ripple in the fabric of space and time.

For them.

We'd heard the stories about him, that he was this crazy guy who lived alone on the edge of town. People called his house, The House of Cards, because of the giant playing cards he'd painted all over his roof. Almost every week someone would drive past and spot him out in his garden dressed in nothing but a G-string. It was Iris who had dared me to take my mother's car so we could drive out there and see him.

'There was a reason I got molested... it made me a genius... a lightning rod like Einstein,' he told us when we got out of the car. 'Did you know that Einstein was really stupid? He couldn't even tie his shoe laces, he couldn't tell the time, but he could see the universe spread out like a snapshot, a brilliant blinding snapshot. And Mozart was like that, his symphonies came to him, fully formed like manna from heaven. He didn't make them up.'

'Really?' Iris said. She turned to me and I had to look away in case I burst out laughing.

'Yeah,' he said.

'And what can you do like Mozart?' she asked him.

'I talk to God.'

'What does he say?'

'He tells me not to worry... would you ladies like to come inside for refreshments?'

I looked at Iris. Our eyes meeting like they were two eyes instead of four. Our eyes always merged like that, as if we were the same person.

'Okay,' Iris said.

'Do you like flowers?' he said as we walked past his flowerbeds. We both had to stop ourselves laughing, which was hard as Iris kept digging me in the back. 'These are my gardenias.'

He'd taken margarine containers and cut them into flower shapes – like big round sunflower heads glued to metal stakes. He'd painted them bright lilac, pink and yellow with Day-Glo fluorescent poster paint. The stakes were driven deep into the heaped-up soil of the flowerbeds.

26

'They're very colourful,' Iris said and touched me on the back, lingering, a long stroke down my spine. I turned my face away, my hand pressed tight to my mouth.

'Is she okay?' he asked.

'She's got a cough, she'll be fine,' Iris told him.

'I've got cough medicine in the house... by the way I'm Ray Meakin Jones.'

He was standing close to Iris, watching me. His shorts, slung so low I could see wiry black hair poking over the waistband. His chest, bare and brown and wet with sweat as if he'd been working hard on something. He had the kind of eyes that some men have that you don't want to look into, milky blue, flat, unreadable, they sent a shiver across my back. I imagined him thinking about our heads like those margarine containers, slitting them and peeling up the skin into a gardenia shape and painting us with Day-Glo paint, and suddenly I didn't feel like laughing.

When he turned his back I whispered, 'He's a freak, let's get out of here.'

'We can take him,' Iris whispered and jostled me, and all the fun came back. She was good at bringing the fun back when I got serious. Moody, she called me. She rarely got moody, she was usually the same, laughing at everything with that sweet smile on her face that her mother said could melt butter when we did something wrong.

When he walked into his house it was like Doctor Who had disappeared into the Tardis, or Doctor Dolittle had climbed into that huge pink snail on the river Amazon. When we followed him in, I could feel chambers disappearing everywhere – rooms sprouting – walls cut into and knocked through, half finished with the plaster and the particle board and all the stuffing showing. It was a crazy, disorienting feeling standing in that hallway. You couldn't get a grip on it. It had the feel of a Fun House at the fair – a brightly coloured maze you could get lost in. I imagined a giant pink snail sailing up a brown snaky river – Rex Harrison's China blue eyes, smiling out. But it felt dark like all that colour was hiding something. I knew there would be rooms that I wouldn't want to see into, locked doors with ugly things behind them, sacks strewn over the floor and stacks and stacks of girlie mags. The sacks all churned up in one corner of the room, where he'd curled up in them – where he'd made his nest.

I felt like my sister Ruby had felt when she first walked into Iris's house. Ruby had turned white and fallen on the ground. She said she had a vision of a man blowing off the top of his head with a shotgun. I asked her what he'd looked like, but she hadn't seen his face. I imagined Iris's father, he was the kind of man you could picture putting a gun in his mouth.

Walking into Ray's house gave me that same feeling, like something was going to happen, or maybe it had already happened; all these things bursting in your head that you didn't want to see. And Iris behind me, pushing me in the back, poking her fingers under my ribs and laughing, almost exploding with the craziness of stepping over the threshold.

'Come in here girls!'

I didn't know where he was but I could hear him shouting.

'I'm in the kitchen!'

Iris pushed me forward, a hard jab between my shoulders.

'Follow his voice.'

But I didn't want to follow his voice. I wanted to run.

She pushed in front of me.

28

When I walked into his kitchen it looked like he'd shattered hundreds of mirrors; the table and the cupboard doors, every surface was embedded with tiny mirror mosaics. When I leant in close to the cupboard doors I could see all three of us reflected a million times like in the eyes of a fly.

Iris was asking him questions, pretending she was interested, pointing at things and asking about them as if she was taking him seriously. She was only pretending to be kind, she always did that, but I knew she wasn't kind. I knew she'd screech and laugh over everything he'd said when we left his house. I knew she'd scorn him for slavering over her like men always did. For wanting to be with her.

'In Kew Gardens there's a white ladder that spirals to the roof of the Palm House. A wrought iron, circular staircase with lots of fancy fretwork twisted through it... it's a ladder to nowhere, the metal steps end just inches before the roof of the domed hot-house,' Ray said.

Ray Meakin Jones. When he'd said his name I remembered that serial killers always had double barrel names, like John Lee Harding, or John Wayne Gacy, or Wilbur Lee Jennings.

I imagined ladders to nowhere sprouting in all of the rooms of his house. Ladders that you'd climb up and not knowing that they just ended, you'd fall off the top and break your neck. I imagined him making Iris climb one of them, her face hot and wet and slicked with tears as he climbed up behind her, trying to force her off, and me feeling so bad that I couldn't save her. Watching her fall and knowing I'd be next.

'What's the use of a ladder to nowhere?' I asked him.

'All ladders lead to nowhere,' he said.

He turned back to Iris quickly, 'Have you ever heard bamboo crack in the rainforest? It cracks through its sheaves as it grows, it just forces its way through. I always think it's what a soul would sound like if it made a sound, because that's what my soul has felt like whenever it has flexed or stretched. I've felt a splinter in my chest, each time my soul has grown.'

He had his hand on his chest, splayed out and suddenly twisting up over his heart like he was really feeling something stretching and cracking.

Iris was listening to him, smiling at him. Fooling him. I knew she wouldn't be drinking in this shit, but I could see that he thought she was drinking it.

I shuddered when I looked up at the painting above the refrigerator, there was no mistaking what it was even though I'd never seen a man's one, but an asshole is the kind of thing that you never really have to see to know what it is. And there it was, right in my face, blown-up huge, more terrible than his peeled margarine containers – graphic, pink, hairy and red. I knew it was *his* asshole, there was no mistaking that. And it wasn't just an asshole, a fly was painted on it, crawling down over a giant hair, like in The Land of the Giants, moving down to the dark red centre, the dark vortex that swirled in the middle of the painting. It made me think about the way a fly moves over things. The way they scurry around looking like they've got no purpose, like they're just running anywhere, taking off in all directions without any aim just all these impulses that are being fed through their tiny fly brains. Moving fast and stopping, testing, tasting, rubbing scents furiously between their legs.

I felt queasy. Sick. I looked away.

'Asshole,' I whispered.

He looked at me, and I knew he didn't like me. I could feel him imagining what my head would look like on a stake.

'Here in the asshole of the world it begins with holes. That's what I paint,' he said.

Iris was staring at his painting as if it was a landscape, as if she was admiring a view.

'It's just ugly,' I said.

But he wasn't listening to me.

'Are you famous?' Iris asked.

Yes! In police files, I thought. I could see his identikit picture rolling out of a fax machine somewhere as we spoke. *This is the perp who was last seen with the two girls*, some hard-boiled, cigar chewing detective would spit out of the side of his mouth. *The Gardenia girls*, that's what they'd call us. They always gave the victims of multiple crimes a fancy name, a name romanticised for the public – the press were like that. But it kind of softened it in my mind. I knew they'd given some of the women serial killer's flower-names like, The Black Dahlia. It made the killer sound more interesting, but it wasn't fair on the victims. I didn't want to be a Gardenia girl.

Those Gardenia girls, beautiful girls they were.

The hard-boiled cop would be standing in the middle of Ray's kitchen, his eyes would drift up to the painting on the wall and there'd be two painted assholes, two tight pink assholes side by side. The assholes of the Gardenia girls.

'A critic called me, the painter of holes,' Ray said. 'He wanted to box me in, to sum me up in a sentence and make my work easy to dismiss. But I liked it, I took it as my own, now I call myself The Painter of Holes.'

'The Painter of Assholes,' I said and laughed, expecting Iris to laugh but she didn't. She was just ignoring me like I wasn't in the room. She was listening to him. Leaning on the bench beside him, looking up at him, her eyes on his face while he kept jumping from one thing to another.

When he talked it was like everything was on the surface, everything blurting out of his mouth, talking about things that everyone else kept quiet about. In my family nothing was on the surface and I knew it hadn't been in Iris's, except for Leo – Iris's twin – who'd just start talking to people about anything that was going through his head, as if he made no separation between people he knew and those who were strangers. All of his words flying out fast, coming out scrambled.

My mother had been making breakfast for me and Iris when the squad car had pulled up outside the house. Iris had looked at me and we'd said 'Leo' at exactly the same time. I can still hear how it came out, it was the eeriest sound, our words meeting like that. And then when we got to Iris's house they'd cut him down and wouldn't let her see him.

I remember Iris's parents, especially her father, breaking down when he left the house for the funeral, his face so red and totally wet, wailing. And that was the terrible sight, not Leo in his coffin who looked happy for the first time in his life.

Iris had turned her face away from me in the car on the way to the service, she'd hardly said a word. But what I remember most was the rope on the top of the piano at the church, it was the strangest thing seeing it there, that someone had either left it there or put it there and had been so thoughtless or deliberate. Iris had nudged me and pointed even though it was the first thing I'd seen when I walked up the aisle, and we'd looked at each other for a second and started to laugh. Then Iris began to cry and after that she didn't stop for hours.

I knew she felt guilty that Leo was dead.

She never liked the way he was, she didn't want him coming in her room when I came over, she always locked him out. She'd shout at him through the door to go away. He'd talk to us, sit there with his back against the door and just babble. Knocking his head every few minutes to remind her that he was there.

She told me that when they were younger, he was always swallowing things like balloons and toys, and everything would stop in the rush to the hospital. I imagined Leo turning blue, lips purple, goggle-eyes bulging.

He was always choking. Iris told me, he scalded himself in the tub and the skin fell off. It smelt like sausages in the car on the way to the hospital.

I imagined sausage meat, boiling pink, boiling red – skin falling from him in big strips. She said it was like he was never really here in the world, he hadn't been meant to live. She told me that even her father had said it. She said once, when she heard Leo choking in his bedroom, she'd walked in and had seen her father just holding him on his lap, not doing anything, just watching him. She shouted for their mother and then the rush to hospital had started up again like it always did.

I remember feeling Leo there sometimes when I sat with my back against Iris's bedroom door. The heat of him coming through the wood and the silence, Iris pretending he wasn't there on the other side when he'd given up speaking, when he'd given up asking to come in. I remember once when I was alone with him, he'd shown me his jars of coloured water, rows and rows of them on shelves in the garden shed. All of the jars ordered in gradations of the same colour. All the reds together, lined up from dark to light, lighter and lighter still, until there was barely any colour at all. He showed me how to make one, loaded his brush with blue paint then dipped it in the clear water. We'd both watched as it spread in paler and paler clouds, until it became the water, until it had all merged together, until it had become its new colour.

My mother had told me to make sure I was never alone with him, she said he wasn't right in the head, but anyone could see that. I'd never felt afraid of him. He reminded me of one of his colours, the palest one, the barely-there one. I knew my mother thought Leo was a dark blob, a black daub – a loaded brush. But he wasn't like that at all. His brush had not been loaded enough and he was always going to slip back into nothing – become clear.

Iris was listening to Ray, she hadn't pushed or elbowed me for a long time so I prodded her in the flesh at her waistband. She turned to me and told me to be quiet. She shushed me.

'Don't shush me,' I said under my breath. I didn't want Ray to see us fighting. I didn't want him to think he could split us up. 'Let's go home,' I told her. I took her arm, tried to lead her. She pushed my hand away.

'Are you in an exhibition?' Iris asked him.

'I don't do that anymore.'

'Why not?'

'Because I don't want to explain myself and people always want you to explain.'

'Explain what?' Iris asked him.

'A stranger stepped out of a flowerbed just as it was going dusk, just as I'd walked outside the toilet, and he told me he wanted to show me something exciting and I believed him. And now I paint holes.'

I knew that I would never have believed a stranger in a flowerbed. But Iris was looking at him as if she believed him.

'You have to grab something before you fall, because we all fall, and grabbing someone in that fall, that's what it's about,' he said.

He was getting out of control. I could see his pupils moving from side to side really fast.

'It's about holding a drunk as he pisses himself dying on a train, in your arms... holding someone you never expected to hold,' he put his hand on Iris's shoulder and she didn't move away.

'Sometimes there's something trying its best to keep you alive... stopping you from just exploding,' he said, almost whispering it to her, his lips so close to hers. His hand slithered up to her throat.

I felt the skin crawl up the back of my neck. My limbs heavy as if I was paralyzed. I wanted to scream but my lips were stuck together, someone had pumped Jell-O into the kitchen and we were no longer breathing air. And then we were running, Iris pushing me along as I ran down the narrow hallway, barely enough width for one person to move along, like a rat in a maze. It was like no hallway I'd ever seen before, a hallway without end, it seemed like it would never stop. I could hear Iris laughing as she pushed me along.

'Don't stop, don't stop!' she was shouting.

I could hear him laughing too, behind Iris, behind us both. Shrieking loud as if it was a game, as if he wasn't chasing two terrified girls through the rooms of his house. But I wasn't laughing. I knew he was pawing her and pulling at her and she was laughing and squealing and trying to push in front of me in that crazy house – through all those crazy rooms – so that he would be behind me and she would be in front. I wouldn't let her pass. I was running, looking for the door, but I couldn't see a way out.

And then the corridor opened up into the space before the door. I could hear him laughing behind me. Iris tumbled in front of me onto the floor. He leapt on top of her, straddling her and she was giggling up at him.

'He got me in the flowerbed and he made me pull down my pants and…'

I screamed at him to shutup, I didn't want to hear it.

'Get off her!' I tried to drag him away from Iris. I tried to pull him off her.

'No, no, you don't understand, that thing that happened to me was like a light exploding in my brain… I can't really explain it, but I think that trauma lights up your brain like a light bulb, one of those huge ones you see hanging on squid boats, a wild bolt of electricity passes through it and lights it up, touching every cell, changing the whole structure of the brain, changing it for the better.'

I didn't think he was telling the truth about it changing for the better, but I knew something had exploded in his brain, I didn't want him anywhere near Iris. I kicked at him to get him away from her, but Iris was just lying there on the ground, looking up at him.

I grabbed her arm and pulled her up, dragged her through the doorway, over the grass into his flowerbeds, our feet sinking in the dirt as I pulled her over to the car.

'Because that's how I feel!' he shouted over the fence. 'Because that's what I felt… high, ecstatic, higher than a kite!' he shouted over the tops of his strange Day-Glo flowers that almost came up to his waist.

'He needs locking up,' I told Iris as I reversed the car so fast away from that fence, away from that house, away from those terrible flowers – wheels spinning in the gravel.

And later, when I drove back along that road, I thought about her there, living in that house with Ray. I couldn't really imagine what kind of life they had. Sometimes when I drove by I saw them out in the garden and I'd pretend I hadn't seen them, like I'd just been driving past, in a hurry, on my way to somewhere else.

Crash Test Dummies

V ICTOR FELT STRANGELY ecstatic when he saw a hand reach underneath the metal grill of the ticket booth. The hand lay still for a few seconds in the smooth depression worn into the counter before a ticket was slipped between its fingers by a hand with long tapered fingernails. He wondered what colour the nails were painted but the film was in black and white.

The film merged with another about a man who worked in a factory that made plastic crucifixes. He checked the quality on the production line as they cooled from the extrusion machine that spat them out. Some of them were mangled: Jesus hideously melted when the plastic hadn't formed properly. It was the checker's job to sort the damaged ones into a box to be remelted and sent back into the machine. But every so often he put a deformed Jesus in his pocket. He took it home and nailed it on his bedroom wall with all the other melted ones he'd saved from the machine.

Victor enjoyed the close-ups, they looked like versions of The Scream by Munch. Jesus's mouth drooping, flowing down towards his chest. Hideously rearranged, shoulders dangling on his cross. Various permutations of his hands joining his torso, seared to his hips, his thighs. Burned and twisted and browned, no longer the pure, pink Jesus that was supposed to come out of the machine.

If there were no perfect things in the world there'd be no one stood at a production line having to sort things out, Victor thought. If there were no lines or fences between things, no cages at the zoo, the doors would just spring open and all the lions and tigers would come running out. He'd like to see a lion roaming the streets. But nothing out of this world ever came around the corner. When it rained it stopped. When the sun came out it went in again. The sun didn't bake you and the rain didn't soak you for forty days and forty nights like the bible had promised.

He wished it would rain for forty days and nights. He'd like to see how the world would look drowned. He could sail up Main Street in a boat holding his plastic crucifix, his deformed Jesus out in front of him, proclaiming the goodness of his journey, the purity of his heart. Hailing the natives who'd line up on the banks as he sailed past, bearing gifts; shiny deformed beads and melted crucifixes. He'd toss them out and their hands would joyously take them, seeing no difference between a good one and a bad one because when the world gets new like that there are no distinctions.

Or maybe he'd strap a large melted Jesus to the helm of his boat like they did on old fashioned sailing ships. But he could only remember women with bare breasts on the prows of those ships. Women were banned from them because they brought bad luck, but sailors put them on the prow to bring them luck.

It was a crazy world but not crazy enough.

~

'Why don't you go on safari if you want to see a lion?' the hairdresser said.

Victor watched her in the mirror as she bent over the top of his head, separating a section of his hair with her comb, preparing to trim the ends. She was very young, probably seventeen or eighteen. An apprentice, a hair-sweeper who had just been given the green light to cut and style.

He always chose a female hairdresser. He liked how they pressed close, seemingly oblivious to the contact. He liked feeling the warmth through their thin clothing, the pressure of their torsos, the occasional brush of their breasts. The touch of a nurse, a dental assistant – clean and warm with no emotion.

'There are no surprises on safari just clichés and Americans,' he said.

'I saw a photo of Japanese businessmen on safari, they were lined up on the back of a Land Rover wearing SARS masks.'

'I like that.'

It was a weird image, he filed it away, maybe he could use it in his work.

'If I went to Africa I'd wear a space suit like the bubble-boy so I wouldn't catch any of those horrible diseases.'

He stared at her in the mirror until she glanced up at him. He held her eyes.

'Don't deny you're beautiful.'

'Beautiful?' she laughed.

'Yes, beautiful.'

'I'm not beautiful.'

'You are absolutely beautiful.'

'I'm not beautiful.'

'What's your name?'

'Sheena.'

'Sheena… own it, don't deny it, and don't let anyone tell you you're not beautiful.'

She looked at him in the mirror, uncertain now.

'No one tells me I'm not.'

~

Victor's flatmate, Gregg, trapped the seedheads of dandelion flowers in shiny resin. When Victor walked around the city he saw groupings of Gregg's paperweights in shop windows everywhere. Little glistening colonies suffocating nature. Victor was sure that when the paperweights were left alone they reproduced, and one day the whole world would be filled with Gregg's translucent moon globes.

Gregg would stride out of his studio in the warehouse they shared, kitted up in his protective suit and industrial visor like he'd just got back from outer space. A great waft of chemicals filling the flat when the door opened.

Victor had never told him that he'd made the same things as a child in his grandmother's shed wearing no protection at all. He could still remember the smell: hessian covered walls, damp raincoats and bird shit all mingled with the toxic smell of resin.

Victor's grandmother had bought him a modeling kit for his birthday. The kit came with small plastic moulds in different shapes. Victor would pour a layer of Epoxy resin into each mould, allow it to set, then he'd arrange shells and bones and feathers on the hardened layer. When he was pleased with the composition he'd pour a final layer of transparent resin over the top. Drowning the objects, forcing out any air. Sometimes the air bubbles got trapped as they tried to escape, he liked it when that happened. It looked like the things had struggled to live on, breathing inside the plastic. He made key rings and paperweights. A brooch for his grandmother embedded with shells that looked like pearls, nestled on a pigeon feather.

In his grandmother's shed he'd fallen in love with making things. He'd experienced a feeling of completeness, disappearing into something fully for the first time. And the rewards had been great: impressing his grandmother, his school friends. Bringing something new into the world that no one had ever seen.

And now he made papier-mâché heads: waist-high sculptures coated with shellac that looked like they were shedding or growing their skin – he didn't know which. He created a translucent effect from building up thin layers of papier-mâché. He lit them from the inside with an electric light, giving them the appearance of being alive at the centre – a shiver under the surface of an insect body. The heads had no eyes, just wide open mouths, all of them the same twisted shape. Arranged in a line on the floor of his studio, they had the callous, blind beauty of sentinels.

He'd started making them after the crash. A three car pile-up that had cracked his skull and scrambled the bones in his body. It had taken him a year of physical therapy to begin to live what people call a normal life. Going back to his studio had been the hardest thing. That first day he'd fallen to the floor and wept. He'd sat for hours staring at his materials thinking he'd never make anything again. He'd tried to reconnect with the desire he'd had, but he couldn't remember how he'd felt before the crash.

He knew that once it had felt like breathing, but that had been when he was a child. He'd kept coming back, sitting on the floor and feeling empty, until the idea for the heads came. He'd seen them first like clowns in a row at the fair, pivoting slowly, their eyes sightless, their mouths red and open, beckoning punters to land a ping-pong ball inside. The image had stirred him and he'd begun to make the heads.

His Car Crash Heads had caused a sensation when he'd first exhibited them. People had read so much into them. The open mouths, the missing eyes, the speechlessness of them – like mute witnesses to a catastrophe. But when he'd kept exhibiting exactly the same sculptures, he'd failed to get another exhibition.

A curator at his last exhibition opening had asked loudly if he could do her one in red. He'd told her that red was too obvious for his Car Crash Heads. That they came in shit brown and shit brown only and she'd have to fucking live with that. But he couldn't make them any differently. He'd tried to think about them in another way, using different materials, but they came out exactly the same. He couldn't make his hands do anything else.

~

'They're all heads,' Sheena said when Victor turned on the lights. Harsh fluorescence lit up the dark corners of his studio.

'I know, I can't seem to stop making them,' he'd intended it to sound witty but it just sounded tinny and strained.

They both stood there awkwardly.

She had a bruised sluttish look that he always found attractive. Her cardigan was buttoned up her spine. All of her clothes seemed put on backwards – in a hurry – like she'd just fallen out of bed and dressed in the dark. He'd waited for her until she'd finished work. They'd kissed a couple of times at the bar, merged together without much purpose then broke apart. She'd smiled at him thinly after each kiss.

He moved close to her. He smelled the chocolate-flavoured martinis she'd been drinking at the bar. She turned away slowly as if she was gliding, as if her head had separated from her body and was moving off in front of her into the room.

'Do people buy them?' she asked doubtfully, staring at the heads.

He pictured one of his sculptures in a suburban lounge, staring out with flat, pebble eyes at some fat guy in a vest wolfing his TV dinner while he watched his favourite sitcom.

'Not lately.'

'How much do you sell them for?'

He knew she wouldn't believe him.

'Sculpture is very expensive.'

'What are they about?'

He shrugged, 'I started making them after I was in a head-on collision.'

'God… did anybody die?'

They always wanted to know about the deaths. It was the first question they asked. People never said: did anyone survive? Are they okay? How do they live after something like that? Not one person had ever asked about the survivors.

'Three people.'

A mother, a father, a child. A whole family wiped out in a station-wagon.

'You were the lucky one?'

He nodded. He didn't like talking about the crash, but he knew other people wanted to talk about it. It was inevitable when they saw the heads. In their eyes he saw the fascinated stare of rubber-neckers. People who had never been in a major crash, who hadn't experienced the brutality of it, always wanted to know the body count. Had he seen a decapitation or someone die in front of him? Had the police carried off a head in a body bag? They wanted all the gory details, but the truth was he really couldn't remember much at all. He sometimes made things up, changed the numbers that had died. He'd make up whole scenarios about heroic acts and people behaving badly, he'd done that a lot when he'd first exhibited the heads.

He didn't want to talk about the crash.

'I went to see a film before I came to see you,' he said.

'Which one?'

He watched a crucifix melt in his head, like a candle collapsing fast on time-lapse photography.

'It's about a guy who works in a factory that makes plastic crucifixes. He sorts out the damaged ones and feeds them back into the machine, but sometimes he puts the melted ones in his pockets when no one is looking and takes them home.'

He hoped she would tell him something. That sometimes she saved hair from her clients, hair that was unusual or had caught the light in a certain way when she'd been cutting it. That she saved it in a piece of newspaper and folded it into the pocket of her coat. She took it home and pressed it between the pages of a book and treasured it; and after everyone had gone home, after she swept the floor and was closing up, she'd sometimes stare for hours at the clippings heaped on the floor – black and red and gold mingling with platinum blond.

46

'Was it a thriller?' she asked.

He laughed, then realised she wasn't joking.

'No it wasn't.'

'What happens in the end?'

'Nothing happens. He nails them to his walls. He lies on his bed and stares at them.'

'He doesn't kill anyone?'

'Not even himself.'

'He sounds like a creep... I thought he'd turn out to be a serial killer. I thought he'd have one of those little darkrooms with photos all over the walls of girls with their eyes scratched out.'

He suddenly felt very angry at her.

'He values them when nobody else does. He cherishes them...'

'Was it in black and white? I hate movies in black and white, I just think, what's the point?' she made a face as if she was sucking a lemon.

He wanted to hurt her. He wanted to embarrass her. But more than anything he wanted her to understand him.

'Because things seem much more close in black and white. The detail moves out from the background and becomes important. Because there's a place where they make crucifixes and rosaries and crazy, cactus Christmas tree lights. There's a place where they make cocktail umbrellas and souvenirs. Where ashtrays shaped like Australia are spat out and cooled on conveyer belts. All the places where the lines have to match up and the words have to be right. Because there are factories where men visit the toilet after they've put things down their trousers. They pull them out and look at them, run their fingers over the damaged things, the things that are not quite right and have a kind of beauty. A new beauty, a melted beauty.'

Sheena stared at him for a few seconds then burst out laughing.

'I worked in a factory and they'd just laugh at you if you said something like that.'

~

'A hairdresser,' Gregg said.

Victor knew what he was thinking. He didn't need to say anything else.

'What happened to Alice?' Gregg said. 'The dancer from Pure Grace, didn't she used to go out with Adrian Fischer? Isn't she Marilyn Chambers's niece?'

Everyone had to be connected for Gregg. Linked in a web that centred around the arts. Six degrees of separation, and everything and everyone had to be cool. Even his moonlighting job making the moon globes was seen as cool – an ironic, knowing wink to the souvenir trade. Gregg wrote blurbs about placing them in gift shops, how he was disrupting the boundaries of what was thought of as a souvenir and what was art. In his real work, as a sculptor, he made giant souvenirs, creating an ambiguity around the objects by blowing them up a thousand times their natural size and positioning them in his installations. And he was lauded for it. Victor wondered why Gregg was still living with him, now that he was seen as such a loser.

'Alice wasn't interested in me, she just wanted to screw a player,' Victor said.

'I thought you were keen on her.'

When Victor had brought Alice back to his studio she had cooed over his sculptures. She'd dribbled her enthusiasm over them. Isn't that what people did to win each other over, Victor thought. Enthused over something, anything, showing each other how much they were connected to life. That they were passionate about something even if it was fake.

Alice had lifted Auden off the bookshelf and read out one of his poems: Icarus taking a tumble in Breughel's painting; the boy falling out of the sky while everyone else continues on with their mundane life. The peasant steers his plough, the fisherman tends his net. A ship sails past, oblivious to the disaster.

She'd told him how much she loved Auden, drinking wine too fast, taking big swigs with that terrifyingly bright smile fixed to her face. He knew if she had a few more she'd dissolve into a crying jag. She would expect him to comfort her, but it would just be a facsimile, a stand-in for understanding. She'd think that they'd moved to a deeper level. She'd go home nursing the fact that he'd consoled her on the couch, and then he'd get her phone call after a suitable interval – he knew she'd play it cool. He'd called her the day after and made it clear that nothing would happen between them. He'd stopped it in its tracks.

Victor wondered how Gregg thought he knew anything about his feelings for Alice. He couldn't imagine Gregg really thinking about him deeply at all. He saw himself pinging through Gregg's head, bound up in a connecting fabric of the school he'd been to, and who he'd fucked, and who he hadn't fucked, and who he was going to fuck; where he'd exhibited, and where he was going to exhibit, and if he'd get there before Gregg. A spiraling DNA strand wriggling through his head. Perhaps it was all the toxic fumes from exploding seedheads in the resin, perhaps there were so many holes blasted in Gregg's brain that everything else slipped through.

Artists were supposed to be the trailblazers, the people who suffered to bring things back from the darkness for everyone else, but most of them were shallow. Often they went to art school because it ran in the family, like becoming a doctor because your father had been one.

Victor had struggled at art school. He'd never felt like he belonged. He didn't speak the right way, he didn't come from the right place, he wasn't embedded in the right fabric; the one that everyone talked about and expected you to belong to. There was so much that people like Gregg took for granted.

Victor had been raised by his grandmother who'd worked in a factory, welding pipe-fittings on a production line. His grandmother, whose photograph had appeared in the local paper when she was a young woman – the miniatures that she'd painted set out on the sideboard in her mother's house. Staring out from that photograph as if she could never quite believe that things could happen. Staring out at him as if she knew everything would be taken away.

Art school had been full of pretenders like Gregg who would sneer at a hairdresser. Gregg should have been licking their feet. His carefully distressed bed hair was always styled within an inch of its life. If spiders made nests that's what they'd look like: sticky and matted and hardly there at all, dull grey and see-through, something you'd see floating in soup in a Chinese restaurant.

'Does this hairdresser do anything else?' Gregg said.

'She does hair. She sculpts it. She uses her hands to cut it and colour it. She makes thousands of tiny decisions every single hour of every day.'

'I was only asking.'

'I'm in love with this woman.'

'You've never mentioned her before.'

He saw Sheena's moon face, her cardigan buttoned on backwards. The muddy brown strip of regrowth in the centre of her scalp. Dull eyes staring back at him. Slack mouth opening – the mouth of an eel.

'We're engaged,' Victor said.

~

Three of Gregg's huge resin globes were positioned around the gallery. Victor stared through the bluish resin at the figures trapped inside. A pair of shop mannequins embedded within each globe: a man and a woman, their clothes flowing backwards, making them look like they were being pushed by a centrifugal force. The woman's hand stretched out as if she was trying to attract someone's attention. Gregg had trapped air bubbles floating out of their mouths, cartoon speech bubbles forever caught in the act of speaking but saying nothing. It was clever, and Victor knew how hard it was to create the effect at that scale.

They reminded him of the line-drawings that had been sent into space to communicate with alien civilizations, but in those images the man's hand was making the gesture. In Gregg's sculptures the man was inert, his arms stiff at his sides. There was something creepy and cold about mannequins and they seemed creepier and colder set in the resin.

The positioning of a body could speak volumes: a hand, a finger, could say so much. But there was a dead feeling about the sculptures. The documentation of ennui. The documentation of emptiness. Why was so much art about the meaninglessness of life, Victor thought? The drawings that had been sent out to alien civilisations held more hope in them, more authenticity than anything he'd seen recently in a gallery. They were from a time and place where people weren't ashamed of imbuing something with meaning. He was tired of seeing meaning punctured. He wanted something to hold onto. He wanted to see something that would move him to weep, something that would make him fall to his knees and change his religion. A lion moving towards him around a corner. A crack opening in the earth. Something that would fill him up instead of drain everything out of him or make him snigger slyly. He was sick of sly laughter. He was sick of irony. He was sick of it all, sick of the heads, sick of making them, he couldn't even bring himself to make one more batch.

One more batch.

He couldn't believe he'd thought about them like that. The production line felt closed.

'Still making those crash test dummies?'

He heard a voice behind him. It was Jeremy Black, a photographer who'd made a name for himself manipulating photographs of horses galloping in moody landscapes.

Before the invention of photography, painters had painted horses galloping with all their limbs in the air. It was a photographer who discovered that one of the horse's hooves was always on the ground. A photograph brought them down to earth, placed one foot on the ground forever. And Jeremy had cleverly redressed the balance, in a series of photographs he'd set the horses free again by lifting them off the ground.

'We've all been waiting to see where you'll go next,' Jeremy said.

'I can't stand the pressure.'

Jeremy laughed as if Victor had made some kind of hilarious joke.

Victor felt his eyes well-up with tears, but he could see that Jeremy hadn't noticed. He wondered what would happen if he started sobbing in front of him, if he just stood there and broke down. If he fell to the floor and wept at his feet, if he shouted, Jeremy! Please help me!

He'd probably think it was performance art.

'Are you working on anything?' Jeremy said.

A melted Jesus loomed in his head. A huge cross and a boat on a journey up a brown, snaky river that looked like the Amazon. Maybe he could make tableaus of himself in various poses, holding a melted crucifix in front of him like the life-size nativity scenes he'd seen in churches. He saw himself captured in a thousand snapshots, his mouth open, screaming. His face wet with tears, weeping. Jeremy could photograph him weeping. Falling to his knees, open and empty and cried-out with the purity of exhaustion. Washed clean.

He wished he was back in his grandmother's shed arranging tiny feathers in the resin. He could see his fingers moving things around, he could see his small face lost in concentration.

'I'm going to sail up the Amazon in a dugout canoe with Sheena my wife,' Victor said.

'I didn't know you were married.'

'She's fourteen years old. She's my cousin.'

Jeremy nodded as if it was the most natural thing in the world. 'Taking some time out, that's always a good idea.'

'We're going to sell shiny beads to the natives. We're going to start a new religion.'

'That's great, Victor... Isn't that Alice Chambers over there? Excuse me.'

And then he was gone.

Victor felt as if he'd been left standing at the water-cooler in some faceless office somewhere. He felt like he should adjust his tie, clear some phlegm in his throat, go back to his cubicle, walk steadily down the corridor giving nothing away and sit down slowly at his desk.

He saw the woman's hand reaching out from the centre of the globe. Inside the resin the silence would be engulfing, squashing everything out like the silence after a crash. That moment when the steering wheel hits and all the air is knocked out of you. The long pause before you take your next breath.

You're going to be ok, son... just breathe slow and steady. We're here for you now, son... everything's going to be alright. The firemen had kept saying over and over, like actors in a corny disaster movie; the kind of clichés that rescue workers always say in those films. And it didn't really matter what they were saying, they could have been making noises like Moomintrolls, or Clangers whistling and singing out from craters on the moon.

Acknowledgements

With thanks to Short FICTION, The Flosca Anthology, The Warwick Review, Cadenza, JAAM, and Landfall.